D1373063

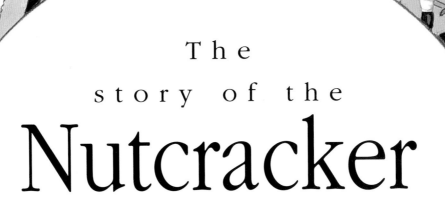

The
story of the
Nutcracker

From a fairy story by E. T. A. HOFFMAN
retold by ROBERT MATHIAS

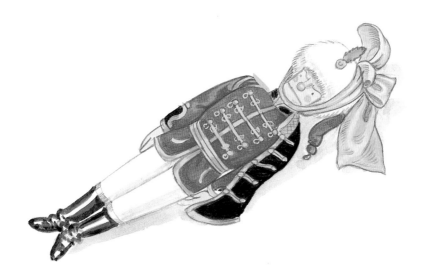

Illustrated by ROBIN LAWRIE

Derrydale Books
NEW YORK

A TEMPLAR BOOK

This edition published by Derrydale Books,
distributed by Outlet Book Company, Inc., a Random House Company,
225 Park Avenue South, New York, New York 10003.

Devised and produced by The Templar Company plc,
Pippbrook Mill, London Road, Dorking, Surrey RH4 1JE, Great Britain.

Edited by A J Wood
Designed by Mike Jolley
Printed and bound in Malaysia

ISBN 0-517-06694-7
87654321

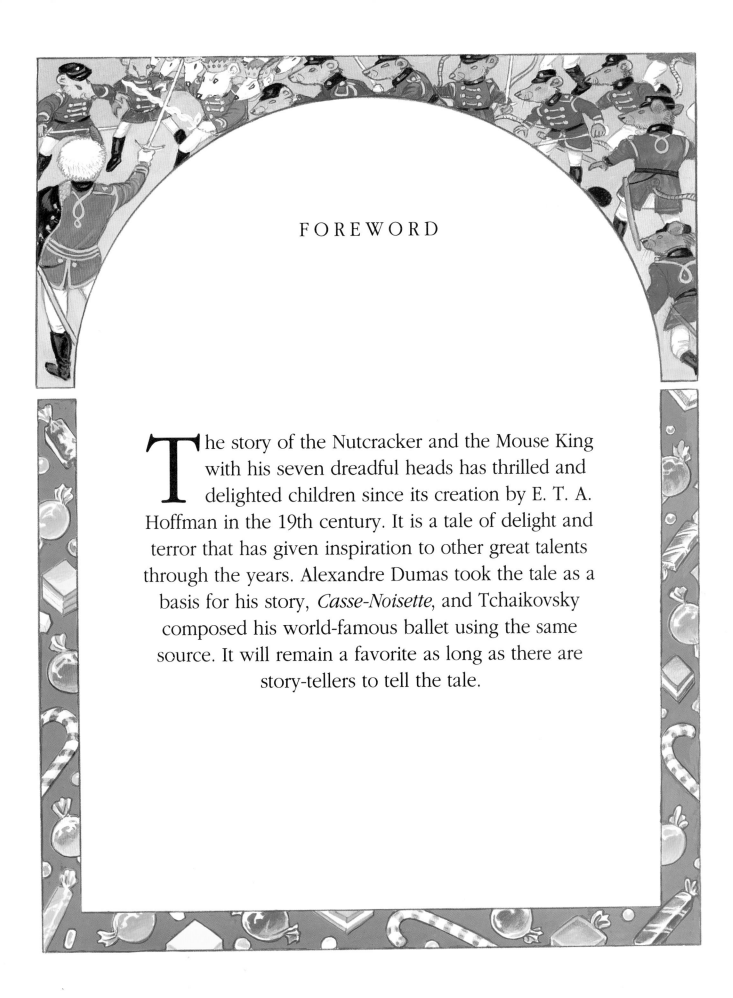

FOREWORD

The story of the Nutcracker and the Mouse King with his seven dreadful heads has thrilled and delighted children since its creation by E. T. A. Hoffman in the 19th century. It is a tale of delight and terror that has given inspiration to other great talents through the years. Alexandre Dumas took the tale as a basis for his story, *Casse-Noisette*, and Tchaikovsky composed his world-famous ballet using the same source. It will remain a favorite as long as there are story-tellers to tell the tale.

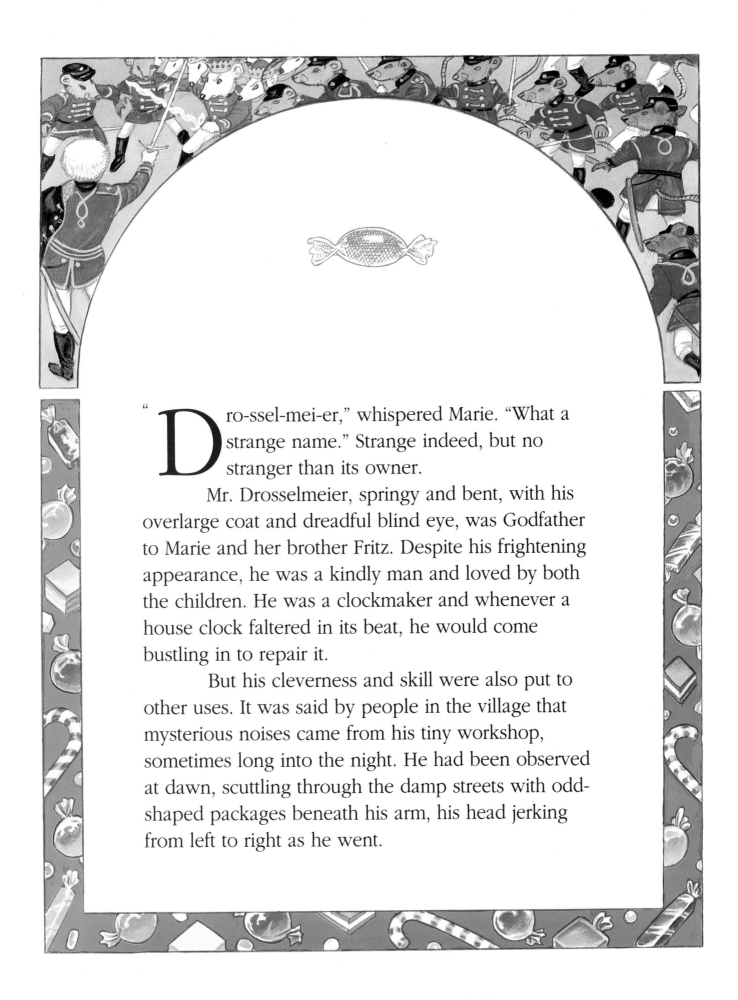

"Dro-ssel-mei-er," whispered Marie. "What a strange name." Strange indeed, but no stranger than its owner.

Mr. Drosselmeier, springy and bent, with his overlarge coat and dreadful blind eye, was Godfather to Marie and her brother Fritz. Despite his frightening appearance, he was a kindly man and loved by both the children. He was a clockmaker and whenever a house clock faltered in its beat, he would come bustling in to repair it.

But his cleverness and skill were also put to other uses. It was said by people in the village that mysterious noises came from his tiny workshop, sometimes long into the night. He had been observed at dawn, scuttling through the damp streets with odd-shaped packages beneath his arm, his head jerking from left to right as he went.

Tonight was Christmas eve and Mr. Drosselmeier had just arrived – cradled beneath his bony elbow was just such a package.

The impatient children waited outside the living room where Mr. Drosselmeier and their parents were preparing the Christmas tree. At last, the door was flung open and Fritz and Marie rushed into the room. The tree was a beautiful green and gold pyramid, blazing with a hundred tiny candles. Its branches were hung with silver and gold apples and colored sweets of every shape and hue. Perched at the very top was a special fairy made from a sugar-plum.

Marie unwrapped her present – a magic
theater with tiny figures of Columbine and Harlequin.
It had a tiny stage and curtains that rose and fell at the
touch of a lever. Fritz saluted his new regiment of
soldiers, neatly boxed in scarlet and blue. There were
horsemen and foot soldiers, each with a silver sword
and rifle.

Hidden in the shadows beneath the tree stood another figure – the contents of Mr. Drosselmeier's strange package. Marie lifted it into the light.

It was a carved wooden soldier made by her Godfather – a hussar in brilliant uniform. His head was large with a strong jaw, but his kind face was curiously handsome. He had a short body balanced on stubby legs. Yet despite his odd stature, Marie thought him very smart. On his head he wore a tall officer's hat of white fur and his scarlet tunic was richly encrusted with gold braid. His white breeches were tucked into shiny black boots.

"What a handsome fellow," said Marie, lifting him up. At once, Mr. Drosselmeier sprang to her side, glad that his latest creation was being admired so by his Goddaughter.

"Ah, but watch this, my child." There was a faint click as he lifted the collar of the soldier's tunic. The strong jaws snapped open revealing two rows of sharp white teeth. Mr. Drosselmeier popped a nut between the teeth and – snap! The hussar promptly split the nut in two.

Marie was enchanted. She examined the hussar's uniform and operated the snapping teeth. But her enthusiasm was too much for Fritz. He had tired of his soldiers and he snatched the Nutcracker from her grasp. Forcing a huge nut between the soldier's jaws, he wrenched at the tiny collar. Three white teeth clattered to the floor and the Nutcracker's jaw hung loose and twisted.

Marie snatched back the wounded hussar and cradled him in her arms. She took a ribbon from her hair and bound up his injured jaw. Fritz, ashamed, returned to play with his army.

Time passed and Mr. Drosselmeier took his leave. The children put away their toys, arranging them in a tall glass cabinet that stood against the wall. They kissed their parents goodnight and went off to their beds.

Marie did not feel sleepy at all. She watched the moonbeams peeping through the curtains. The snow piled up on the window-sill cast a blue glow into the room. She thought about all her toys and decided that the Nutcracker was her favorite. She wondered if he was lonely, locked in the tall cabinet, and decided to go downstairs.

She got out of bed, pulled her robe close
about her, and tip-toed down the stairs. The house
was very still and dark and at the foot of the stairs she
shivered. She crossed the hall and, as she took hold of
the living room doorknob, the great grandfather clock
at her side whirred and struck the hour. Her heart
jumped and she stood there, frozen to the spot. She
turned the doorknob as the clock chimed twelve times
– it was Christmas day.

Marie entered the darkened living room. She opened the glass cabinet and lifted down the moon-grey figure of the Nutcracker. She looked into his brave green eyes and placed him back on the shelf next to her favorite doll. Her trusted teddy bear was placed on his other side. Silently, she closed the cabinet and turned to retrace her steps.

Curiously, the room seemed larger and the darkness between herself and the door had become a black chasm. She stood very still, a chill shiver creeping up her back. Then she heard a noise – a rustling, scampering, scurrying noise that grew louder until it filled the whole room.

Marie held her breath and her heart pounded wildly. She peered into the blackness – tiny pin-pricks of light began to appear all around her. The lights were in pairs – a hundred pairs of tiny, shining eyes were staring at her. Everywhere she looked there were mice with gleaming eyes creeping closer and closer.

The mice formed a circle in front of her. Then, to Marie's horror, a dreadful squealing filled the room. A gigantic mouse, a hideous creature with seven hissing heads, was squeezing up through the floorboards. Each evil head wore a spiky crown and each spiteful mouth was drawn back in a snarl to reveal vicious yellow teeth.

It was the Mouse King.

Marie was terrified and dared not move. The Mouse King held a fearsome sword, twisted and stained from a thousand battles. He swung it high over his head and the army of mice formed into ranks behind him. Marie stepped back and fell against the cabinet. Her elbow struck the glass and shattered one of the panes. As she fell to the ground she heard another sound, quiet and urgent:

Come awake this night,
To fight, to fight.
Show steel, not fear,
The Mouse King's here.

Marie looked up and saw that her toys had come to life on the shelves of the cabinet. The dolls were huddled together behind the teddy bear who stood bravely in front of them, looking anxiously down at the scene below. They clung together in fright, but striding along the shelf, his silver sword held high, was the Nutcracker. His broken jaw seemed mended now and his handsome face wore an expression of calm determination.

"To arms! To arms!" he called and Fritz's regiment of soldiers tumbled out of their boxes and hurried after him.

The Nutcracker leapt down from the cabinet and charged at the mouse army. His foot soldiers knelt in rows and fired off their muskets, smoke puffing from the tiny barrels. On either side the cavalry spurred on their horses and galloped towards the angry mice, their sabers scything the air. The two armies clashed and Marie watched as they engaged in a terrible battle.

The Nutcracker was fearless, calling out
commands to his troops as he slashed and parried
with the angry mice. Suddenly, his attention was
diverted for a split second, and he was pounced on by
a dozen ferocious mice. They pinned him down and
thrust him back against the wall.

The Mouse King seized his chance. He sprang at the Nutcracker, his soiled blade raised to deliver a fatal blow. Marie screamed a warning, but the Nutcracker did not hear as he struggled to rid himself of his attackers. He broke free, unaware that the Mouse King's sword was slashing through the air towards his heart.

At the last moment Marie tore off her slipper and hurled it at the seven dreadful heads. Her aim was true and the slipper found its mark. The instant it struck the Mouse King, the moon seemed to disappear behind a cloud and a strange silence filled the air.

Just as quickly, the moonbeams lit the room again but, to Marie's surprise, everything looked as it had when she had first entered the room. The mice were gone and the toys were all back in their cabinet. The house was silent once more and Marie fell senseless to the floor.

In the morning Marie awoke to find her
mother next to her bed.

"Are you all right, my dear?" she asked, her
voice full of concern. "I can't imagine what came over
you last night. I heard a noise at midnight and found
you lying on the living room floor. You had cut your
arm. And what a mess there was! The glass cabinet
was broken and there was blood and broken glass all
around you."

Marie's thoughts returned to the dreadful battle of the previous night. The figure of the Mouse King reared up in her memory.

"Is the Nutcracker hurt?" she asked. "Is he alive? And the soldiers – are they safe?"

Her mother smiled.

"What a dream you've had. You must have cut yourself falling against the glass cabinet. It's early yet. You should get some more rest, my child, before the excitement of the day takes over."

And as soon as Marie closed her eyes she drifted off to sleep.

Marie woke suddenly to the sound of a soft tap, tap, tap on her door. She got out of bed, dressed quickly and opened it. Her mouth fell open in surprise – standing in front of her was a handsome prince, dressed as a hussar. He looked exactly like…

The Nutcracker smiled and took her hand.

"Dearest Marie," he said. "I give you my warmest thanks. Last night you saved my life. When your slipper struck the Mouse King it broke the spell he had cast on me. I am no longer a toy, I am as I used to be and free to return to my palace in the Kingdom of Sweets."

He drew her closer to him. "It is such a land of sweetness and beauty, I would be honored if you would agree to let me show it to you?"

Marie smiled into his handsome green eyes and nodded her head. She held on tightly to the prince's hand as he lifted her off the ground. They floated out of the window and high into the sky. Higher and higher they went and Marie looked down at the streets of the village and the tiny people scurrying about their business.

Soon, the village was far behind and they were drifting over a thick forest. The tall, snow-clad pines on the higher slopes seemed to reach up as if to touch them. It began to snow but Marie didn't feel in the least bit cold.

All around her the snowflakes swirled and danced. Marie looked closer and then laughed out loud – they really were dancing! Indeed, each and every snowflake had turned into a tiny fairy, dancing delicately in the crisp morning air.

Marie and the prince flew on above the winter
landscape, the snow fairies skipping around them.
Suddenly, the fairies moved apart and a tall, slender
figure drifted towards them. She was dressed in a pure
white robe trimmed with snow-white fur. On her head
she wore a tall crown, fashioned from ice and set with
the palest sapphires. The Snow Queen smiled at the
prince who bowed politely. Marie curtseyed and took
the Snow Queen's outstretched hand.

"Come," said the Queen. "I will help you on
your way."

Immediately the snow fairies swooped down and formed themselves into a sleigh made entirely of ice. It took the three passengers high over snow-capped mountains and sheltered valleys where tiny villages huddled away from the wind. At last they glided down between the tall pine trees and landed on a wide, frozen river.

"This river will lead you to the Kingdom of Sweets," said the Queen.

Marie took the prince's hand and stepped out of the sleigh. As her foot touched the ice, the Snow Queen, the sleigh, the snow and the river all vanished. Marie found herself standing in a sunlit meadow speckled with wild flowers of pink, yellow, scarlet and blue. Looking closer, Marie was amazed to find that they weren't flowers at all – they were sweets!

"This is Candy Meadow," said the prince, "and over there is Sugar Wood."

They walked across the meadow and as they
entered the sun-dappled wood, Marie noticed that the
trees were covered with sugar-fruit blossoms. They
swayed in the breeze and tinkled like tiny bells.
Further on, they came to a dancing, bubbling river,
perfumed with the scent of citrus.

"This is Lemonade River," laughed the prince,
smiling at Marie's astonishment.

Hand in hand, Marie and the prince walked along the banks of the tumbling river. She was no longer surprised by the magic delights of this enchanted land. Tall sugar rushes grew in clumps from the marzipan banks; clusters of crimson jelly-fruits and yellow marshmallows dotted the cotton candy bushes, and outcrops of honey-colored toffee pushed through the sugar-spun grass. Beneath their feet was a pathway of caramel squares, each one neatly sealed with peppermint cream.

At last they came to a clearing in which stood a spectacular palace, gleaming like gold in the morning sunshine. Silver gates hung from barley-sugar columns and a wide terrace of pink candy steps led up to the doorway.

They entered the palace and its beauty filled
Marie with wonder. The floor, polished and shining,
was a mosaic of fruit sweets, richly patterned in
turquoise and gold. Slender columns of ivory icing
soared up to a molded ceiling where flowers and
animals, noblemen and ladies were delicately carved
in snow-white sugar. Everywhere you looked, there
were golden bowls of delicious sweets.

In the great hall were two splendid thrones
made of crystal mint hung with peardrops. In front of
each was a marshmallow footstool. On the wall
behind the thrones hung a huge tapestry, its rich
pattern woven with spun sugar. The prince and Marie
took their seats and the prince rang a tiny silver bell.
Immediately, the hall came alive with dancers.

To begin with came maidens and milkmaids, dancing with herdsmen and hunters. Then a high-stepping Spaniard came stamping and stretching, followed by a gilded Sheik who shimmered like the desert sun. Next, came bobbing, silk-wrapped maids from faraway China, as pale as porcelain, smiling and leaning like reeds in a breeze. A bounding, leaping Cossack whirled and flew like a top across the floor and dizzied the watching assembly. He was joined by a team of laughing children in colorful costume who linked arms to march around the hall.

Then the crowds drew back and a whisper ran around the hall. Marie clapped her hands in delight as in danced a sugar-plum fairy. She floated and lifted as if she was thistledown blown on a summer's day breeze. Around and around the great hall she danced, entrancing all who watched her delicate ballet.

When her dance was over, the prince took Marie gently by the hand and led her down to the ballroom floor.

"May I have the pleasure of this last dance?" he asked as enchanting music once again filled the hall.

Marie closed her eyes as the prince waltzed her around the room. She was so happy as she danced in his arms that her feet felt as light as a feather. Her ears were full of sweet music and her senses reeled with the perfume of a thousand blossoms. But gradually the music and the perfume faded, drifting away as she spun in a whirl of happiness. She could feel instead the warmth of the sun on her face.

Then came a thud and a tumbling bump.

Marie opened her eyes. She was back in her bedroom, sitting on the floor beneath the open window. The morning sunshine was streaming in on her face.

"Dear Nutcracker," she murmured. "He has brought me safely home."

And, smiling happily to herself, Marie prepared to dress, as from downstairs came the sounds and smells of Christmas day.